He's the Prince of Pranks!

PRINCE JAKE

Monster Madness

FOR ALL THE CHILDREN OF
NEWBRIDGE PRIMARY SCHOOL –
HOPE YOU LIKE THIS ONE!
S.M.

FOR MY OTHER LOVELY NIECE,
ROBYN
M.B.

ORCHARD BOOKS
338 Euston Road, London NW1 3BH
Orchard Books Australia
Level 17/205 Kent St, Sydney, NSW 2000

First published in 2008 by Orchard Books
First paperback publication in 2009
Text © Sue Mongredien 2008
Illustrations © Mark Beech 2008

The rights of Sue Mongredien to be identified as the author
and Mark Beech to be identified as the illustrator of this work
have been asserted by them in accordance with
the Copyright, Designs and Patents Act, 1988.
A CIP catalogue record for this book is available from the British Library.

ISBN HB 978 1 40830 278 1
ISBN PB 978 1 84616 615 0

HB 1 3 5 7 9 10 8 6 4 2
PB 1 3 5 7 9 10 8 6 4 2

Printed in Great Britain by
CPI Antony Rowe, Chippenham, Wiltshire

Orchard Books is a division of Hachette Children's Books
an Hachette Livre UK company.
www.hachettelivre.co.uk

He's the Prince of Pranks!

PRINCE JAKE

Monster Madness

SUE MONGREDIEN MARK BEECH

ORCHARD BOOKS

CHAPTER ONE

"Pssst! Over here!"

Prince Jake jumped. He'd been rushing across the Great Hall with his brother and sister, on the way to breakfast, and the urgent whisper had taken him by surprise. "Who said that?" he asked, gazing around.

His brother, Prince Ned, pointed up at the stuffed head of a wild boar that hung on a wall nearby. It had bulging eyes, long sharp tusks and matted hair. "I think it was *him*," he said in alarm.

Jake rolled his eyes. "Don't be daft!" he said. "Stuffed animals don't—"

"Psssst! *Here!*" came the whisper again.

"It's definitely that warthog," Ned said nervously, stepping back.

Princess Petunia snorted, sounding very much like a wild boar herself. "For starters, it's a *boar*, not a warthog," she said. "And it's been dead about two hundred years by the looks of it."

"If anyone knows about *bores,* it's you, Petunia," Jake said, dodging out of the way as she tried to swipe him.

"Stop bickering!" the whispery voice came again. "It's me, the King!"

Jake stared around the Great Hall. As well as the wild boar, he could also see a stuffed stag's head on the wall, a few ancient, moth-eaten tapestries, and marble statues of various royal relatives...but there was no sign of his father. "Where *are* you?" he asked, feeling confused.

King Nicholas wasn't exactly the smallest of people, after all.

There was a rustling sound and suddenly the King stepped out from behind a large wall-hanging. "Over here," he hissed, beckoning them towards him. "Quick! Before your mother sees us!"

"Oh, I get it," Petunia said, walking briskly across the stone floor. "This is about tomorrow, isn't it?"

Jake scrunched up his face in a frown. "Tomorrow?" he echoed, following her.

The King dragged them all behind the wall hanging, which smelled of mould.

"Oh, yeah, course," Ned said, grinning. "Dad's checking we haven't forgotten. As if we'd dare!"

"Forgotten what?" Jake asked, still not understanding. "What are you on about?"

At Jake's words, all eyes swivelled towards him.

"He *has* forgotten," Petunia said, folding her arms and looking disapproving.

"Oops!" Ned giggled, his eyes round. "You haven't *really*, have you, Jake?"

"Er...course not!" Jake blustered. He didn't have a clue what they were talking about, but he got the feeling it was something major. "Just winding you up. As if I'd forget an important thing like...like that!"

His dad looked at him suspiciously. "Glad to hear it," he said, after a moment. "So – what have you all got for her, then?"

Got for her? Got for whom? Wasn't anyone going to explain what this was all about?

Petunia tossed back her long blonde hair. "I've ordered a new rose garden to be planted," she said, in a smug voice. "The flowers are just about to come into bloom – and they'll spell out M-U-M."

Jake bit his lip. M-U-M? But Mother's Day had been ages ago!

"Very tasteful," King Nicholas replied. "She'll love it. Boys? How about you?"

"Um..." said Jake, stalling.

"I've got her a new horse," Ned said proudly.

"Splendid!" King Nicholas boomed, slapping his youngest son on the back, before remembering they were supposed to be whispering. "I mean...excellent," he added in a low voice. "That will go perfectly with the new stable block I've had built for her!" He turned to Jake expectantly.

"And Jake. How about you? What treats have you got lined up for your mother's birthday tomorrow?"

Jake felt a stab of guilt. Uh-oh. Mum's birthday was *tomorrow*? Why hadn't anybody reminded him?

The King leaned a little closer, his eyes

twinkling. "We can always count on you for something really special, I know. The karaoke machine at Christmas, and the giant squid to go in the royal lake for her last birthday...very original, Jake!"

There was a swift tip-tapping of footsteps just then, and the King peeped out from behind the wall-hanging. "Here she comes!" he hissed.

Jake, Ned, Petunia and the King all huddled under the musty tapestry while the Queen walked through the hall.

Jake's mind was racing. Yikes. Mum's birthday. He was going to be in big trouble if he didn't give her a present. What was he going to get her?

When the Queen's footsteps had died away, the King pulled back the tapestry, and they all stepped out.

"Better go to breakfast," Jake said quickly, moving away from the others before they could see the guilty look on his face. "Don't want Mum suspecting anything."

"But you haven't told us your present!" Petunia put in, hurrying to catch him up.

Jake scowled at her. There was no need for her to look *quite* so smug! "It's a secret," he muttered. He walked as fast as he could away from them all, to avoid any more questions. He *had* to come up with a present his mum would love – and he had to come up with it fast. But what *did* you give a queen who already had everything, anyway?

CHAPTER TWO

Prince Jake racked his brains all the way through breakfast. He barely noticed his food, he was thinking so hard. But the number of brilliant present ideas he came up with was precisely...none.

"You're very quiet this morning, dear," the Queen said, walking around the table to put a hand on Jake's forehead. "You're not coming down with anything, are you?"

For a millisecond, Jake was tempted to fib and pretend he was suffering from something serious and contagious. Maybe that way, he could spend tomorrow in bed and avoid the whole present-giving thing…

Then he remembered the horrible royal nurse, Mrs Botch, and her bottles of disgusting medicine. "No," he replied reluctantly, spooning in another mouthful of crownflakes. He gazed out of the window and pretended to be interested in the royal gardener who was trimming one of the hedges into a peacock shape.

"Just...just thinking."

"Mmm, I wonder what about," his dad teased, waggling a bushy eyebrow up and down. "Can't imagine *what* our Jake could possibly be pondering on right now, eh?"

Jake gritted his teeth, trying to ignore his dad, who definitely seemed to have sussed him, worse luck. Jake smiled sweetly at the Queen instead. "Actually, I was just looking forward to your birthday, Mum," he began. "And I was wondering—"

Princess Petunia tittered behind a perfectly manicured hand. "Here we go," she said in a loud whisper to the King.

"I knew he'd forgotten," the King snorted, spluttering on his gold-plated cup of tea.

Jake glared at them, before giving his mum another wide-eyed smile. "I was wondering...what you're hoping to get?"

Petunia gave a hoot of laughter.

Prince Ned coughed loudly, with the word "Forgotten!" somehow coming out in the cough.

Queen Caroline sipped her coffee. "You know me – I love surprises," she said. "Something unusual would be wonderful."

"If you've really forgotten, you can share my present," Ned whispered helpfully to Jake. "But you can give her the bottom end, all right?"

Jake scowled at his brother. Like he wanted to give their mum the back end of a horse! He wasn't that desperate! "I *haven't* forgotten," he hissed. "And I told you, anyway, it's a surprise!"

The Queen, overhearing, raised her eyebrows at Jake's fierce tone of voice. "Sounds wonderful," she said. "I'm looking forward to it already."

That morning, Jake, Ned and Petunia went along to the school room for their lessons as usual. Their governess, Ms Prudence, was already at the blackboard, chalking something up, as they sat down at their desks. She turned to greet them, and Jake saw she'd written "Mythical Creatures" in large letters on the board. He tried not to sigh too hard as he took his gold pen and leather-bound exercise book from his desk. The Prune, as he and Ned called

Ms Prudence, never taught them anything *useful* like Birthday Present studies, or Surprise Gifts: The Top Ten, or…

"Jake! Are you with us?" The Prune's voice cut into his thoughts and he raised his head from where it had sunk onto his desk. "I said, who can tell me what a mythical creature is?"

Petunia took out a pot of bright pink nail polish and started painting her nails. "Dragons and stuff," she said. "Weird, ugly creatures…like snotty little brothers."

Jake flicked the lid of his pen at her and she jumped and splodged nail varnish all over her thumb. *"You're* the only dragon

round here," he said, sticking his tongue out at her.

"That's enough!" the Prune snapped. "Now, we're going to be starting a new project on myths and legends, and I thought it might be fun for us to study some of the more unusual creatures. Dragons, phoenixes, griffins, the sphinx..."

Petunia let out a bored sigh, but Jake and his brother exchanged excited glances. For once, one of the Prune's lessons actually sounded all right!

"To start us off, I thought it might be fun for you each to dream up your own magical creature," the Prune went on. "Make it as weird and wonderful as you wish. What does it look like? What can it do? Where does it live? I want you to write all about it."

Jake gazed out of the window, and started thinking up a monstrous creature.

Maybe something with tentacles...yes, that was good. Long, green, squirming tentacles, and red gooey warts on its head. One huge staring eyeball, and a wide purple mouth. It was strong enough to *kill* someone if it wrapped a tentacle around them, and squeezed...

Jake started writing notes as the ideas rushed into his head. The monster ate... well, anything. He glanced over at his sister, who was trying to sneakily put on lip gloss behind her book. It definitely ate princesses, Jake thought, scribbling the words down. And scary nurses. Teachers, too. The monster wasn't fussy, no way. And it lived... Where would it live?

He stared out of the window again, trying to think up the perfect place for his monster to hang out. His gaze fell on the moat below, thick with green pondweed, and he chuckled to himself. Of course! The

monster lived in the royal moat. A moat
monster – perfect!

For once, Jake really enjoyed the lesson,
making up the grisliest, most bloodthirsty
details he could about his moat monster
for the whole morning. The Prune had
them studying Maths that afternoon – or
Princely Sums, as she called it – but after
tea that evening, Jake carried on writing
about his moat monster, and even drew a
gory picture of it biting the King's head off.

"Are you *sure* you're not ill?" the Queen asked, coming in to check on Jake that evening. "You, doing homework, outside school hours... It's unheard of."

"I'm fine!" Jake said, hastily covering up the picture of his half-eaten dad. "I just want to finish my homework."

The King looked alarmed at Jake's words. "I think we should call Nurse Botch," he muttered to the Queen. "Something is *definitely* wrong with the boy."

"No!" Jake cried, jumping up at once. "Look," he said, doing a handstand in front of her. "See? Fine."

He picked up his football and bounced it five times off his head. "See? Fine!"

"All right, all right," the King said, grabbing the football just before it crashed into a chandelier. "Bedtime in half an hour, all right?"

Jake waited until they'd gone, then called through to Prince Ned, whose bedroom was next door. "Listen to this," he said, when Ned had come in. "Oh, hang on," Jake said, flicking on his torch, and turning off the main light. "There – that's better. Good and creepy. Ready?"

Prince Ned wriggled excitedly on the edge of Jake's bed, where he was perched in his Spider-Man pyjamas. "Ready," he replied.

Jake shone his torch onto the page and put on his spookiest voice. "The moat monster has ten tentacles, with rubbery suckers along each one. Every sucker is full of stinky poison, and whenever the monster grabs a victim, poison pours onto the person's skin...and their flesh rots away!"

"Eugh!" Prince Ned cried. "That's disgusting!"

Jake smirked. "The monster lives at the bottom of the moat. When it farts, it lets out big, poisonous bubbles full of smelly gas that kills all the fish."

Prince Ned collapsed in giggles. "No!"

"Oh yes," Jake said, enjoying himself enormously. "And it has one gigantic eye which can see in the dark. The monster spreads out its tentacles, searching for prey. Anything will do. Animals, children, members of the royal family..." He looked up and saw a maid come into the room to hang up a freshly ironed dressing gown for Jake to wear in the morning. "And *maids*," Jake added quickly, hoping to scare her as well as Ned. "It loves chomping up maids."

"And how does it kill them?" Ned asked eagerly. "Does it eat them straightaway, or do that flesh-rotting thing first?"

"It depends how hungry the monster is," Jake said, in a solemn voice. The maid had gone into Jake's private bathroom that led off the bedroom, and he could see her squeezing toothpaste onto his bronze toothbrush for him. "Sometimes, it crushes them to death with a mighty tentacle. Their bones splinter and break, and their insides go all squishy," he added, making up the details on the spot. "Sometimes, it gnaws their heads off with one great gulp!"

There was a nervous laugh from the bathroom, and the maid emerged. "Excuse me, Your Highness," she said. "I've got your hot-water bottle here, to warm up your bed, and..." She broke off and edged closer, clutching the hot-water bottle to her chest. She looked anxious, Jake noticed. "That was a...good story, Your Highness," she added.

"*Story?*" Jake scoffed, thinking quickly. He couldn't resist the chance to try and wind her up. "It's no story," he said, wide-eyed. "There really *is* a monster in the moat. Didn't you know? I saw it myself just this morning! Don't go swimming out there, whatever you do!"

With a muffled scream, the maid shoved Jake's hot-water bottle under his duvet and ran out of the room.

Jake and his brother both burst out laughing. "Fancy believing that!" Jake guffawed. "Classic!"

It was only when Jake was in bed later on that he realised he still hadn't got a thing for his mum's birthday tomorrow. He'd been so busy with his monster that he'd forgotten all about getting her the perfect present – again. And now it was too late to get her anything!

Jake tossed and turned. He was going to be in such trouble! The Queen would be so disappointed. And Jake would seem like the worst prince ever!

CHAPTER THREE

"Happy birthday to you,
Happy birthday to you,
Happy birthday, Queen Caroline
Happy birthday to yo-o-o-ou!"

Prince Jake rubbed his ears. What a
racket! He was surprised the lamps hadn't
smashed, with all that high-pitched
wailing. Who *was* that big fat woman in
the spangly frock, anyway, and what was
she doing in the breakfast room?

The Queen was clapping like mad, with a starry-eyed expression on her face. "Bella Piccolo – what an honour it is to have you here!" she exclaimed.

"My pleasure, Your Majesty," the woman replied, dropping into a deep curtsey. "Many happy returns."

Jake winced at the view of the singer's enormous spangly bottom as it rose and fell in front of him. It was enough to put a prince right off his royal bacon.

The Queen looked dazzled, as Bella Piccolo waddled out of the room. "Darling, thank you," she said to King Nicholas. "My favourite singer, singing me happy birthday... What a wonderful surprise."

"My pleasure," the King grinned. "And that's just for starters. Wait and see what's to come!"

Jake stared down at his plate, not wanting his mum to see the guilty expression on his face. He'd managed to make a card for her this morning, but he *still* didn't have a present to give her. How was he ever going to wriggle out of this one?

Boris the butler wheeled in a great sack full of cards that the Moranian public had sent the Queen. Then Mrs Pinny, the housekeeper, staggered in with armfuls of flowers. "This bouquet is from the

33

Prime Minister," she said, "and there are quite a few others, too, from the Duchesses and Earls, and foreign kings and queens."

"Thank you, Mrs Pinny," the Queen said. "Gosh – it's like having our very own rainforest in here."

"Here's a card from me, Mummy," Princess Petunia said, carrying a large red envelope over to her. "I'm afraid I couldn't wrap my present – too big to get the paper round. I'll take you to see it after breakfast."

"Thank you, sweetheart," the Queen said, hugging her. She opened the envelope and pulled out a gold-plated card with a huge sparkling diamond on the front. "How beautiful!"

Jake looked down at his own card in dismay. It had got a bit crumpled when Nervous Rex had tried to jump on Jake's bed while he'd been drawing it. To make matters worse, Rex had let out a great doggy sneeze on it too, and some of the felt tip had got smudged. It didn't look anything like a *royal* birthday card.

"Here's a card from me," Prince Ned said. "And I couldn't wrap *my* present either. But I drew a picture of him instead – here."

"Oh!" the Queen exclaimed, peering in wonder at the drawing. "Another dog! How lovely of—"

"It's not a dog, it's a horse!" Ned corrected her. "Look, it's got a mane!"

"Oh, yes, of course," the Queen said quickly. "Silly me. A new horse. How wonderful." She opened the card from Ned. It was silver-plated, and studded with lots of tiny, glittering rubies. "How divine," she murmured, turning it so that the rubies caught the light.

Jake looked down at his card once more and sighed. Next to Petunia's and Ned's cards, it looked rubbish!

He took a deep breath. "And here's a card from me," he said, passing it over to his mum. "And...er..." He shuffled his feet, feeling awkward. "And *I* couldn't

wrap your present either," he added,
"because..."

"Because he hasn't bought you
anything yet," Petunia smirked, sticking
out her tongue at Jake.

"Forgotten!" coughed Ned, grinning
at him.

"I *didn't* forget!" Jake snapped. He
turned back to his mum. "I've got you
a surprise," he said. "And you can have
it later."

37

"Thank you," the Queen said, giving him a kiss. "That sounds exciting. You know how much I love surprises!"

Jake gave a weak smile and wondered what on earth he was going to give her. This present was a surprise to *him* as well, right now!

Boris the butler was peering out of the window, his eyes narrowed. "There are an awful lot of helicopters flying around the castle this morning," he said. "Is there something I should know about?"

"News to me," the King said. "Probably the press, trying to get a good snap of the birthday girl. Nothing to worry about, I shouldn't think."

The crystal telephone rang in the corner of the room as he finished speaking. Boris hurried to answer it. "Moranian Castle, Boris speaking, how may I—?" he began, then frowned. "*What?*" he exclaimed.

"Is this some kind of a joke?" He put his hand over the receiver and addressed the table. "Sorry to bother you, Your Majesties. It's a journalist from *The Scoop*. Wants to know if you have any comment on the... er...bone-crunching monster living at the bottom of the royal moat?"

"The bone-crunching *what*?" the King spluttered. "Hang up, Boris, it must be a practical joker. Honestly! Where do these fools get their ideas from? Bone-crunching monster indeed!"

"Oh! It must be—" Prince Ned blurted out suddenly, but Prince Jake kicked him under the table, and shot him a fierce look before he could say anything else.

Like Ned, Jake had guessed *exactly* where *The Scoop* reporter had got the idea of a bone-crunching monster. It seemed that the maid really had believed his moat monster project – and in her fright, had called the newspapers. But he couldn't let his parents find out that the press invasion was anything to do with *him*.

First he'd forgotten to get his mum
a present, now he'd caused this mess!

The phone rang again, and Jake ran to
grab it before Boris could get there.
"Moranian Rainforest, can I help you?" he
said. "Who? Royal family? Wrong
number, mate."

As soon as he put the receiver down, it
rang again. "Moranian Castle, monster
speaking, just eaten the royal family,"
Jake growled, then did an enormous burp
down the line.

"Jake! That's enough!" the King said.
"Those idiots will print anything – we'll
end up with a national day of mourning
if you're not careful!"

The phone rang again and again, and
Boris fielded the rest of the calls. One
journalist after another was trying to get
the exclusive on the monster story. And
the sky was full of photographers in

41

helicopters, buzzing around the castle,
trying to get a snap of the beast!

Queen Caroline tutted in annoyance
as Boris dealt with the tenth reporter
in two minutes. "I wish they would
leave us alone," she said crossly.
"Today of all days. They're such pests."
She glared out of the window at the
helicopters. "And it's Saturday! You'd
think they'd have better things to do."

"They're probably all after a photo of me really," Petunia said, gazing out of the window. "Yoo-hoo! Look, I've had my hair done!"

"Come away from there, Petunia," the King snapped. "If we all ignore them, they'll get fed up with hanging around soon. Now – why don't we give out some presents? That will cheer us all up."

Jake had had such fun on the phone, he'd almost forgotten about his present problem, but at the King's words, his heart sank again. Giving presents to the Queen might cheer the rest of the family up, but it had just plunged Jake right back into despair!

CHAPTER FOUR

Princess Petunia led the whole family
out of the breakfast room, through the
ballroom and outside to the formal
gardens. "Here," she said at last, in a
smug voice. She stopped before an area
the size of a small field that had lines of
carefully planted rose bushes, all spilling
out their sweet smell. There were deep red
roses, bright yellow roses, pale pink roses,
even some weird-looking black ones. And

yes, there in the middle, spelled out in white roses, was the word MUM.

Queen Caroline breathed in the scent, and hugged her daughter. "It's gorgeous," she said.

"I *knew* you'd love it," Petunia said, triumphantly. As soon as her mum wasn't looking, she pulled a gloating, better-than-you kind of face at Prince Jake.

Jake gave her a ferocious monster scowl in return. He was feeling really sick of perfect Petunia today! In fact, if she didn't watch out, she was going to get a shove right into her precious roses. *Let's see how much she's smiling then, with thorns sticking out of her bum,* he thought darkly.

Prince Ned was hopping from foot to foot. "My present next! My present next!" he said. "This way!"

Ned led them through the gardens, across the courtyard and along the side of the royal golf course until they reached the stable block. True to his word, King Nicholas had ordered a whole new extension to be built, and it stood there, the golden roof gleaming in the sunlight. There was a huge scarlet rosette, the size of an armchair, tied across the front archway, and a wide

47

ribbon that stretched all the way around the building.

"This bit is from me," the King said to the Queen. "And Ned's present is inside, I believe."

The Queen's eyes sparkled and she clapped a hand to her mouth with excitement. "Ooh, thank you!" she cried, gazing up at the new building. Then she cut the ribbon across the entrance, and led the family into the stableyard.

"Come on, Mum," Ned said, hurrying past her. "He's over here!"

Alfie, one of the grooms, was waiting with a handsome black stallion in the centre of the yard. The stallion blew down his nostrils as Ned led the Queen to him. She stroked his nose and he harrumphed into her hand. "He is *gorgeous*," the Queen sighed happily. "I can't wait to go for a ride on him!"

"Thought of anything *you* can give Mum yet?" Petunia asked Jake in a too-loud whisper.

"I *have* thought of something to give *you*," Jake growled, giving her a shove. Petunia went flying, straight into a pile of horse poo.

Petunia let out a screech. "Jake! I hate you!" she wailed in horror.

Jake couldn't help laughing. She was covered in sloppy, stinky poo – and it served her right! "Oops," he said, in his best apologetic voice. "Oh dear. It's in your hair, too. Hope the press don't get a photo of *that*."

Petunia screamed at the thought, and the King gave Jake a stern look. "Any more of that, and there'll be no birthday cake for you, son," he said, helping Petunia to her feet.

"Ugh – Petunia stinks!" Ned put in, fanning himself. "Yuck!"

The helicopters buzzed lower above their heads just then, and the stallion shied away nervously.

"Oi! Your Majesties!" came a faint shout. "Any word on this monster, then?"

The Queen glared up at the helicopters. "Are they *still* nosing around?" she grumbled. "Honestly! Don't they have anything better to write about, than some monster that doesn't even exist?"

"Jake's the only monster around here," Petunia muttered, using a tissue to flick the horse poo off her skirt.

"In fact," the Queen went on, "it would be the best present ever, if someone could teach those wretches a lesson!"

Jake's ears pricked up at his mum's words. What was that? The best present ever?

He thought hard. Petunia had just called him a monster, hadn't she? Well, what if he, Jake, could show the reporters a monster?

He grinned as a brilliant idea popped into his head. Yes! There might just be a way! If he could pull this off, he might be able to give his mum a right royal treat after all...

"Mum," he said, "I'm just going to make sure your birthday surprise is all ready for you. Meet me at the top of the basement steps in an hour, and I can show you what it is."

CHAPTER FOUR

At eleven o'clock, as arranged, Prince Jake
met his mum and led her downstairs to
the basement floor of the castle. It was
cool and quiet down there, with a damp
smell lingering around the old stone walls.
The spooky dungeons were in the
basement, as well as twenty or so storage
rooms. There was also the underground
dock, which Jake now led his mum
towards. The dock was where the royal

submarine was kept most of the time. It had often been used as an escape route in the past, whenever the castle had been under siege from invading armies, but nowadays the royals rarely needed it.

"Ooh, this is exciting," the Queen said, as her heels clattered along the stone floor after Jake. Then a suspicious expression crossed her face as they approached the dank, musty-smelling dungeons. "You're not going to lock me in a dungeon or anything, are you, Jake?" she asked.

Jake shook his head. "No – something much more fun than that," he assured her. "We're going for a little ride. Nearly there!"

They came out onto the lower dock, which had a platform at one side, and a sloping runway on which the royal submarine was moored. Jake grinned at the sight of it. Good old Boris had sorted

everything out, just as Jake had asked
him to!

The Queen's face cleared as they stepped
towards it. "A submarine ride?" she asked.
"Is this my surprise?"

"Yep," Jake said. "It was just going to be an ordinary ride," he added hastily. He didn't want her to think he'd only just come up with the idea. "But the press helicopters got me thinking. Those reporters want a monster, don't they? And I reckon that this submarine, covered in pondweed, will look pretty monster-like!"

The Queen's eyes were merry with delight. She giggled. "You mean...we're going to try and trick them?" she asked.

Jake nodded. "That's the plan," he said.

One of the royal mechanics, Bill, stepped forwards and opened the submarine hatch. It lifted with a swooshing noise. "If Your Royal Highnesses are ready, I can take you out for a spin," he said politely.

The Queen winked at Jake. "Oh, I think we're ready," she said. "What are we waiting for? Let's do it!"

Jake and the Queen clambered aboard.
Jake hadn't been in the royal submarine
for a while, and gazed around with
excitement. He had forgotten just how
brilliant it was inside! The walls were lined
with dark red velvet, and a diamond
chandelier dangled from the ceiling.
There were portholes along the sides,
and polished leather armchairs a little
way back.

Bill went into the engine room, and a smartly dressed steward called Ralph showed Jake and the Queen how to fasten the seatbelts in their chairs. "A selection of snacks will be served shortly," he said, with a deft bow. "And the choice of movies today is—"

"We're all right, thanks, mate," Jake cut in. "Bill said we could watch what's going on above us – periscope TV!"

Ralph nodded. "In that case, allow me to turn on the screen for you," he said, leaning across to flick a few switches.

Jake and the Queen watched as a TV screen slid down from the ceiling and came to a smooth stop in front of them. Ralph pointed a remote at it, and it lit up.

"You can't see much while we're sitting here in the dock," he said, as a picture appeared on the screen of some boring-looking pipes. "But when we get out into the moat, Bill will send the periscope up, and you'll get to see the castle, and what's happening around it."

Jake grinned. "We're hoping to surprise the journalists out there," he told Ralph.

Ralph nodded. "Very good, Your Highness," he replied. "In which case, you might be interested in this." He showed Jake and the Queen a long, tube-like microphone, and demonstrated the "on" switch. "If there's anything you'd like to say to the press once we're in the moat, there's a waterproof loudspeaker fixed onto the periscope."

The Queen thanked him. "Very thoughtful, Ralph," she said, then turned to Jake. "This is going to be so much fun!"

A moment later, they heard the purr of the engine, and the submarine began to move through the water.

"This is your captain speaking," came Bill's voice through a speaker. "We have left the docking area, and will be entering the moat any second...now."

Jake wriggled with pleasure in his seat. He was very fond of the moat. It ran right around the castle grounds, and had always been a very useful place to "lose" things he didn't want any more, like homework and sensible vests and...well, all sorts of things, really. And now they were going to ride right around the bottom of it. How cool was that!

The TV flickered in front of them, and

Jake laughed as he caught sight of some surprised-looking fish darting across the screen, through the sludgy brown water.

"The periscope is now going up," Bill announced from the engine room, and the picture on the TV screen began to change. Suddenly Jake and his mum could see the sky, still filled with helicopters. And there, on the banks of the moat, stood journalists, with their notepads and mobile phones. A couple of camera crews were setting up, too.

"This looks a good spot," they heard Bill chuckle. "We're right under a massive clump of pondweed, so I'm going to take the submarine up to the surface and see if we can surprise anyone out there. With a bit of luck, when it's covered with weeds, the sub will look exactly like a big green monster."

Jake could feel the submarine rising up through the moat. And then, on the TV screen he saw one of the journalists open his mouth very wide and point a shaking finger at the moat. Then came a whole series of blinding flashes of light, as the photographers all started snapping away.

The Queen was almost crying with laughter. "They really believe that this is a m-m-monster!" she stuttered, shaking with giggles. "The idiots!"

One of the journalists was crouching at the water's edge, being filmed for a news

programme, Jake guessed. Jake couldn't
resist flicking on his microphone, and
letting out a great monstrous growl.
"GRRRRRRR!!"

The reporter was so startled, she lost her
balance, her arms flailed about...and she
toppled headfirst into the moat!

"Gotcha!" Jake chortled into the
microphone. "One–nil to the royal family!
Prepare to get chomped, lady!"

CHAPTER FIVE

Prince Jake and his mum laughed and laughed as they watched the reporter floundering about in the water, before being rescued by her cameraman. Then the Queen took her microphone. "Time I had a word, I think," she murmured, switching it on. "Good morning," she said into it, in a regal voice. "This is your Queen speaking."

Jake could see the reporters freezing at her words, even the soggy one, who'd been trying to shake off the pondweed.

"Thank you for making this a
memorable birthday for me," she went
on. "As you can see, there *is* no bone-
crunching monster in our moat, just a
rather splendid submarine. I'd be grateful
if you could all leave now, so that I can
enjoy the rest of my birthday in peace."
She paused, watching them on the screen.
They all seemed too shocked to move.

Jake frowned. "You heard her, scram!" he shouted into his microphone. "Before we call the guards!"

The reporters hurried away at once. The camera crews began to pack up and drive off in their vans. The helicopters all buzzed off, too, leaving a silent blue sky once more.

"And good riddance," the Queen said, dabbing at her eyes. "Oh, Jake, that was just the funniest thing I've ever seen."

Bill put his head around the engine room door at that moment. "Now we've got rid of that lot, does anyone fancy having a go at steering the submarine?"

Jake and his mum looked at one another and grinned. "Definitely," they said in unison.

Up in the nose of the submarine, it felt rather like being in the cockpit of a plane, Jake thought, checking out all the switches and levers everywhere. There were two big windows to look through at the front, with a line of headlights shining into the murky water of the moat.

The Queen had first go, as it was her birthday. Bill showed her how to lower the submarine back into the depths of the moat, then how to guide it through the water.

When it was Jake's turn, he slid into the driving seat eagerly. It was so funny, seeing the fish swim past the window and... Hey, what was that? Jake cringed as he caught sight of one of his homework books drifting by, looking very soggy. Oops! Better not let Mum see it!

He steered the submarine sharply to the left...only to glimpse something brown tangled in the pondweed in front of them. Oh no! The hated violin Jake had "lost" in the moat a few weeks ago, when he couldn't be bothered to practise! He really couldn't let the Queen see *that* either!

He turned the wheel hard right, hoping she hadn't recognised it.

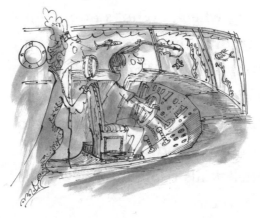

"Careful!" Bill warned, glancing down at the computer system in front of him. A green light was flashing. "You just hit a wall – oh!" He broke off and stared at the computer screen. "Where *are* we?" he murmured, scratching his head.

"What do you mean?" the Queen asked.

"Well, according to the tracking system, we just went right through the moat wall.

We've gone off the radar," Bill said slowly. "Which means..." He shook his head. "No. Surely not."

"What?" Jake asked, gripping the steering wheel. "What's happening?"

Bill stared through the windows in front of them. The Queen and Jake did, too, wondering what was so interesting. The moat seemed to have got very narrow, Jake thought, as brick walls came into view either side of them.

"I think it must be a secret passage," Bill whistled. "I've never seen it before. Where on earth does it go?"

He came and put his hands on the steering wheel, with Jake's. "We'll have to guide this in very carefully," he said, his eyes fixed on the walled sides of the passage. "That's it, Your Highness, nice and slowly..."

Jake held his breath as he and Bill
steered the submarine. After a few
moments, the gloomy passage seemed to
open up again, and the submarine came
to a halt against some kind of stone dock.

"Well, I never," Bill said, shaking his
head in disbelief. He flicked a switch to
make the lights brighter at the front of the
submarine, and the three of them pressed
their noses against the windows for a
better look.

"It's some kind of old vault, by the looks of it," the Queen said, with a thrilled note in her voice. "I've never even *seen* this part of the castle. Shall we explore?"

"Yeah!" Jake cheered. Wait till Ned heard about *this*!

Bill turned off the engine. "Allow me, Your Highnesses," he said, going to open the hatch.

One by one, Jake, the Queen, Bill and Ralph all clambered through the submarine hatch and onto the stone dock. Bill handed out some torches, and Jake wasted no time switching his on and shining it around the vault. It was very high, and at least as big as the Great Hall of the palace. The stone ledge they were standing on ran along one side of the murky vault, with stone shelves built into it. Water covered the rest of the chamber.

"I wonder if this was an old storage vault?" the Queen murmured, pointing her torch up at the stone ceiling. "It would be a perfect place to hide treasure, especially if you thought you might be attacked..."

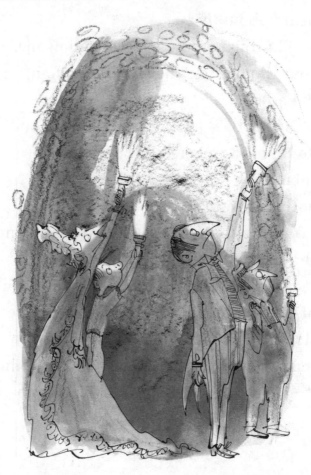

Jake's heart skipped a beat. At the exact moment his mum had said the word "treasure", his torchlight had fallen upon something glittering in the stone wall behind him. He reached out for it, his fingers closing around a cold metal shape, and he shone the torch on it. "Wow," he breathed. It was a ring, cobwebby and tarnished. He wiped it on his top and looked again. It shone bright silver under the torchlight, with what looked like a diamond cluster on top. It even had the royal family's coat of arms inscribed inside.

"Mum – look!" he said, holding his hand out towards her, with the ring in his palm. He grinned. "This is the last part of your present," he told her, as if he'd had it planned all along. "Happy birthday!"

The Queen let out a squeal of excitement as she saw the ring and threw her arms around Jake. "Thank you, sweetheart!" she cried. "Oh, thank you – for all of this!" She kissed him on the top of the head. "This has been the most exciting, unusual birthday surprise I've *ever* had!"

Jake couldn't stop smiling. Phew – he'd pulled it off. There he'd been this morning, worrying that he'd be in trouble and disappoint his mum on her birthday. And now it had turned out to be a monstrous success, after all!

LOOK OUT FOR MORE
RIGHT ROYAL LAUGHS WITH

Sticky Gum Fun
978 1 40830 276 7   £8.99

It's Snow Joke!
978 1 40830 277 4   £8.99

Dungeon of Doom
978 1 40830 280 4   £8.99

Knighty-Knight
978 1 40830 281 1   £8.99

Monster Madness
978 1 40830 278 1   £8.99

Swordfights and Slimeballs!
978 1 40830 279 8   £8.99

Here's a taster of

Swordfights and Slimeballs!

Prince Jake clasped the hilt of the silver sword, his eyes locked on the enemy before him. "You've done it now," he hissed, taking a step forward. "You should never have come here." He raised the sword and pointed it menacingly. "Now it's time to *pay*!"

"Wait!" came the scream. "Please – I beg you! Show some mercy!"

"No chance, loser," snarled Jake. He swung the sword through the air, the heavy silver blade swishing, and...

"Prince Jake! Prince *Jake*! Are you listening?"

Jake jerked out of his daydream just as his sword sliced through an enemy neck and blood splattered everywhere.

Rats.

He wasn't fighting off the enemy after all. He didn't even have a whopping great silver sword in his hand. He was still here in the royal school room, with his governess Ms Prudence droning on.

Double rats!

PICK UP A COPY OF

Swordfights and Slimeballs!

TO FIND OUT WHAT HAPPENS NEXT!